Krysta

Little Bear Finds a Friend

written by Kathleen Allan Meyer
illustrated by Carole Boerke

Library of Congress Catalog Card Number 90-72096
Copyright © 1991 by Kathleen Allan Meyer
Published by The STANDARD PUBLISHING Company, Cincinnati,Ohio
Division of STANDEX INTERNATIONAL Corporation. Printed in U.S.A.

Little Bear held on to his mother's skirt. He refused to go out the front door.

"I don't want to go to school," he said, tearfully, "I won't know anyone."

"Albert and Alfred will be in the classroom right next door," coaxed Mother Bear.

For a moment Little Bear brushed
away his tears. But then he remembered
some things his brothers had said about
school.

"There's too much homework, Little
Bear," Albert had volunteered.

"You must be quiet. You can't make
lots of noise," Alfred had chimed in.

Little Bear started to cry all over again. He turned to Mother Bear, "But who will be my friend?"

"There will be lots of friends for you to meet at school," Mother Bear answered, "but you must remember one thing—to *find* a friend, you must *be* a friend."

Then she slipped Little Bear's backpack over his shoulders.

"*Now* come along," urged his mother, "you'll find some delicious honey sandwiches and a blueberry muffin in here for your lunch."

Somehow that didn't make Little Bear
feel any better even though he usually
loved honey sandwiches and blueberry
muffins. But he knew that when his
mother said, "*Now* come along," it
meant he better do what she said.

Sadly he gave Mother Bear a little
bear hug. Then he started down the path
tagging along after his brothers.

Soon they came to the little red schoolhouse. It looked very big! And Little Bear felt very small!

Alfred and Albert left him at the door
of his classroom. Peeking inside, Little
Bear didn't see one friend. Only the
teacher smiled at him and said, "Good
morning!"

Finally he stepped inside and chose a
chair closest to the door. Then his
mother could see him right away when
she came to pick him up. And he would
see her sooner, too.

Little Bear looked around and saw the
children doing all kinds of fun things.
One was painting at an easel. A boy was
washing dishes with real soap and
water. And two children were planting
seeds.

But Little Bear just sat and watched and waited. He was still afraid! And he couldn't tell which one was his friend.

Just then the teacher came over and showed him a pretty bluebird some of the children were cutting out.

"Little Bear, would you like to take one of these home today?" she asked him.

Feeling somewhat braver, he answered, "Well . . . maybe . . . I think so."

And he was able to cut out his bluebird very nicely.

Just as he finished, the little girl next to him started to cry. She didn't know how to cut out her bird.

Little Bear remembered what it had been like when he had tried to cut out valentines last year for his mother and brothers. He had cried then, too.

"I'll show you how to cut out your bluebird," he offered.

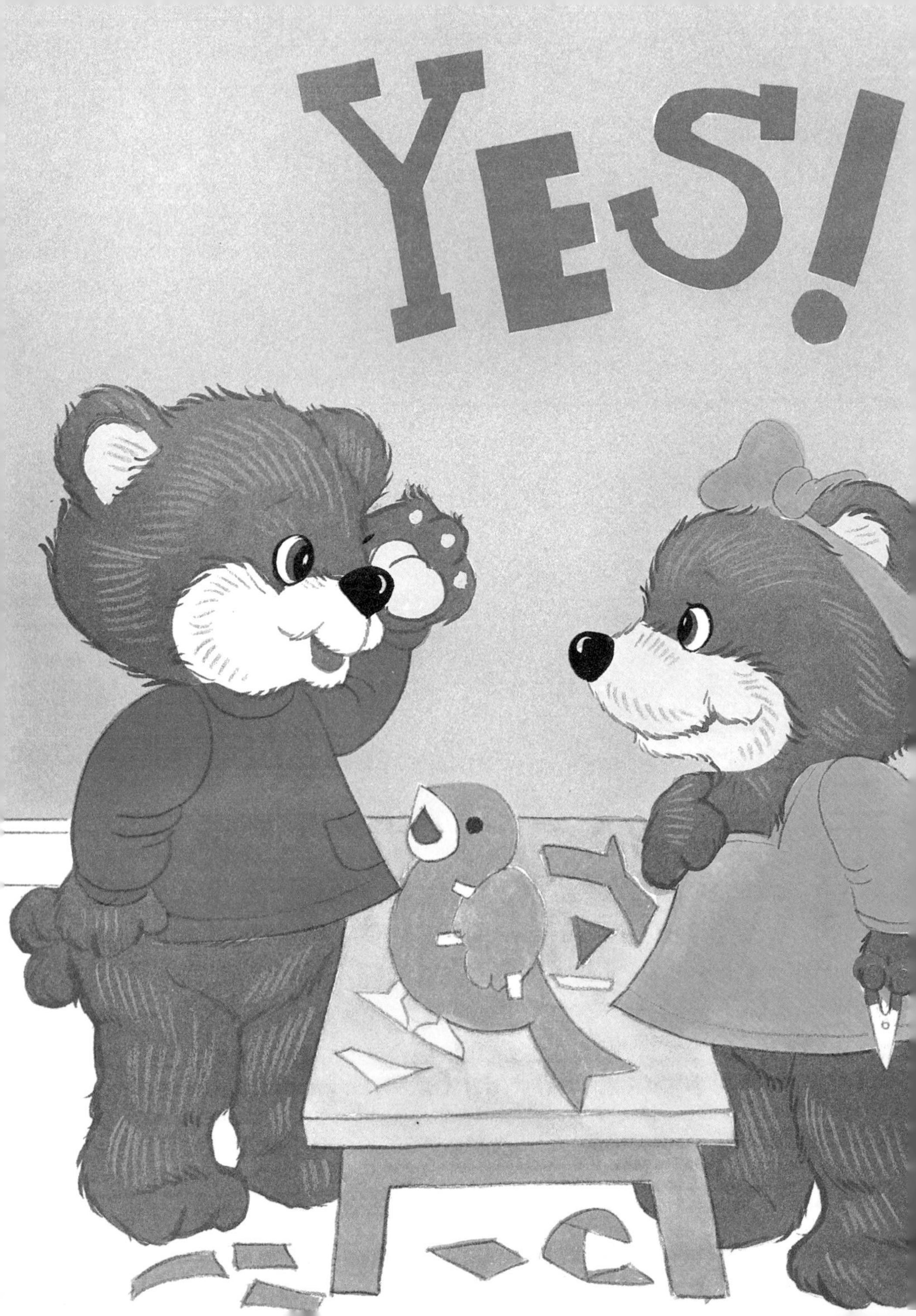
YES!

Between them they soon had the job
done.

"Would you be my friend, Little
Bear?" his new friend asked.

And, of course, Little Bear said a big
loud "Yes!"

That evening after Mother Bear had tucked him in and kissed him good night, he thought about his first day of school and the new special friend he had made.

Mother Bear is right, he said to himself. *Finding friends is easy to do if you remember to be a friend yourself!*